TRICKS, TREATS, & TOUR GUIDES

MAISON DE LOUP

ALSO BY MAISON DE LOUP

Myths in Love

Book 1 - The UnCupid Cupid

Book 2 - Were Without the Wolf

CHAPTER I

CHOOSE YOUR TRAVEL COMPANIONS WISELY

PIPER

I have always been obsessed with Ireland. There's just something about it; I can't get enough. The culture, the language, the accent, the myths and legends. I love it all. It's been my dream for as long as I can remember to travel to the Emerald Isle and live my best Irish life.

I have been saving for this epic adventure my whole working life. Halloween in Ireland, the birthplace of my beloved holiday, is my dream. Yes, you heard that right. Halloween is my favorite holiday. I live my best Halloween life every day. You should see my home decor; my boyfriend hazes me for it.

Zero fucks given.

It has taken me a while to get here. There have been setbacks for sure. Who knew you could break a tooth or two on those cute little candy hearts with the mushy phrases on them? Or that a teenage driver who doesn't quite understand that a yellow light means yield would hit you and total your less-than-a-year-old car?

Then there are all the adulting things no one tells you about. Get a house, people say. Nobody mentions all the things that can go wrong there, nope. Garage doors that come off the hinges, roof replacements, plumbing leaks, the list goes on and on. I've dealt with a good deal.

And don't even get me started about COVID. Years of delay. All of which is to say that the funds for my dream trip fluctuated, and the timeline to go kept getting adjusted.

But none of that matters now.

The moment I look out of the plane's window and see endless green atop rocky cliffs and stormy ocean waters, all the struggles to get here evaporate. My excitement bubbles its way to the surface. I can feel the smile spreading across my face as my heart leaps for joy. I start shaking my boyfriend, Curt, to share the stunning view.

"What?" he grumps beside me.

"Look," I squeak in excitement.

Curt slowly turns and leans over me, peering out the small window. He looks at me and shrugs.

"It's an island," he says, readjusting his neck pillow before closing his eyes. My smile falters at his lack of excitement. Curt knows how much this trip means to me. He wasn't overly excited when I said I was finally ready to book the trip, not that he complained when I paid for his ticket.

He only got a little more enthusiastic when our friends Cate and Graham got wind that we were going on this adventure. Suddenly, my dream vacation with my boyfriend morphed into one where his best friend and his best friend's girlfriend were joining us. Not that I am opposed to having friends along, but the self-invite was a lot annoying.

My bestie Marie had loads to say about that. The plan had always been for her to come with me, but between military life and her growing family, she wasn't able to get away.

I turn in my seat and look at Cate in the row behind me.

"Cate," I say through the gap between the window and the seat. "Cate," I say a little louder when she doesn't answer.

"Cate!" I yell, finally getting her attention.

"What's up?" She asks, setting her phone down.

I point to the window. "Look," I say enthusiastically.

Cate raises her window shade and looks out the window. "Pretty," she says before pressing her phone against the window to snap some pictures.

Deflated once more, I turn back around in my seat, not even bothering to try and get Graham's attention. For people who were more than happy to let me use my rewards miles to cut down the cost of their tickets, another topic Marie had some strong opinions about, no one seems thrilled to be here.

The pilot comes over the speaker system and announces our final approach. As we begin to descend from the sky, I decide I have two choices.

Choice number one: I can let these unenthusiastic dipshits, because that is how I feel about them currently, ruin my vibe. Choice two: I can live my best Irish adventure, and if they are miserable, that's a them problem.

"I thought we were renting a car," Curt complains as we stand on the curb of the airport waiting for our rideshare.

"Like, are we going to have a car at all while we're here?" Cate asks, reapplying her makeup for the third time since we landed. I swear, we spent fifteen minutes waiting for her to come out of the bathroom once we deboarded the plane. When I went back in to check on her, I found her curling her hair with a travel curling iron and half the countertop covered in her cosmetics.

Now she's standing next to me with her perfect figure, blonde hair pulled into a sleek pony, flawless makeup, and a super cute outfit of tight jeans and slouchy sweater with trench coat and fuzzy boots, looking like a model. Even as she continues to wave the still-hot curling iron in her hand to cool it off.

I, on the other hand, have on leggings and a hoodie with my well-worn tennis shoes, no makeup, and hair in a messy bun. Comfortable, but nowhere near model status.

Graham, who has been completely absorbed in his phone, finally looks up. "Guys. We're on vacation," he says with an easy smile, throwing an arm around Curt and Cate. "Let's get to the hotel and grab some drinks. We can figure out the transport situation later."

I want to point out that when I booked, I informed everyone we would be taking the train to travel, but I'm so thrilled with Graham's upbeat attitude, I say nothing.

Curt and Cate both give him a smile and seem to relax. The ride share pulls up, and we load everything, including ourselves, into the car. The ride from the airport to the hotel is short. We check in and drop our bags off, then head out to the nearest pub after Cate freshens up—again.

We grab a table by the window and browse the menu. While the others chat about the "strange" food names and drink options, I sit back and take in the room. A live band plays an upbeat tune in front of a small dance floor. The long wooden bar is packed full, staff busy, bustling down the length and back. I hear the musical, accented language drifting through the air on conversations and from people singing along with the band.

My heart swells to the happy beat. A lovely waitress with a lilting voice comes by to take our drink order.

"First time here?" she asks with a friendly smile.

"Yes!" I say chipperly. "I've wanted to come here my whole life."

"Well, welcome to Ireland. We're happy to have you," she exclaims. "Any fun plans?"

I nod happily. "Yes! We're going to do all the tourist things.

Blarney Stone, Hill of Tara, Jameson distillery, Oweynagat Cave, and end with the Derry Halloween Festival."

"Goodness, that is quite the magical tour! But be careful, Ireland is the birthplace of Halloween. This is the time of the year when the fae will be out looking for innocent humans to lure away and whisk off to the fae realm."

Curt and Graham both snort, and I catch Cate rolling her eyes. If our waitress notices, she gives no indication.

I smile even more than before. "I'm hoping for a glimpse, but I'll be careful not to be lured away."

We give her our order, and she dashes away.

"This is amazing! The music, the pub, all of it," I shout over the rising chorus of voices singing the next tune.

"It's so loud," Cate whines

"Did you actually understand what the girl said to us?" Curt asks skeptically.

"It's," Graham says, looking around, "a vibe. But I bet after a few rounds, it'll be awesome." He shrugs.

The waitress drops off our drinks, and Graham orders another round, with shots. While the others drink and play on their phones, I continue to simply live in the moment, absorbing the music and happy vibe of the pub.

Several rounds in, Curt and Graham head to the bathroom while Cate wanders around the pub taking selfies. I'm still nursing my second drink, head happily bobbing along to the music, when I feel a tap on my shoulder. I turn to find an extremely handsome man gazing at me with a mischievous smile.

His eyes seem to shift in the light, first looking blue, then green. He has a wide, prominent brow and a tapered nose, perfectly centered between high cheekbones along a jaw that looks like it was cut from granite by one of the masters. Waves of copper hair are partially pulled back, leaving the rest to hang loose at his shoulders. Broad shoulders taper down to a narrow waist and fit thighs, all showcased by the fitted polo and jeans he's wearing.

He's not just handsome, he's gorgeous. Yet there's something off that I can't quite put my finger on. There's almost an otherworldly air about him.

Jeez, not even a full day here, and I'm already looking for fairies.

"Shall we?" he asks, extending a hand to me.

I cock my head, confused. "Shall we what?" I ask.

"Go," he says. Ah. Drunk.

I shake my head and offer a smile. "I'm so sorry. I'm here with my boyfriend and friends. Did you need me to call you a rideshare, or do you have friends here who can take you home?"

His smile drops, replaced by sheer confusion. He must be more drunk than I thought.

"You're not coming with me?" He asks, seeming genuinely perplexed.

I shake my head and glance around, hoping to spot someone looking for a missing friend.

"No. I'm good here."

"Who's this?" Curt asks from behind me.

"Oh, Babe. Good. You're back. I think he's drunk. He needs help finding his friend."

The handsome man continues to stare at me as if I'm a puzzle before shaking his head. "I'm good. I'll just...go," he says, backing away.

I watch him back up and disappear into the crowd before turning back to Curt.

"That was odd. Poor guy kept asking me to go with him."

Curt scoffs and rolls his eyes. "Must be wasted. With you looking like that? He had to be."

I glare at my grumpy-ass boyfriend and flip him off.

"I'm just saying," he starts, but is interrupted by the return of Graham and Cate. They are both swaying on their feet with glossy eyes.

"We're gonna head back to the room," Cate says.

"I'll join you," Curt says. "You coming?" he asks me.

"I think I'll stay for a bit."

"Suit yourself," Curt says before heading off with the others.

I roll my eyes and go back to enjoying the music. It's becoming clear that of the two options I thought of on the plane, I am definitely embracing option two. I'm going to live my best Irish adventure life, and if they're miserable, that's on them. Lesson for the future: always choose your travel companions wisely.

CHAPTER 2

I'M BROKEN

LIAM

"**E**smeralda!" I bellow the moment I return to the fae realm. I storm through the long marble hallway towards the main chambers where many of the fae should be gathered.

"Esmeralda, where the fuck are you?" I yell as my wings unfold and begin to vibrate in agitation. Where the hell is our healer?

The fae in question drifts out of a doorway at the end of the hall. "What on earth is the matter, Liam?" she asks, more calmly than the situation calls for.

"I'm broken."

"Broken?" she asks quizzically.

"Broken." I reaffirm.

Esmeralda focuses her sharp purple eyes on me, turning her head this way and that.

"I detect nothing wrong," she finally says.

I pace away from her and back in my frustration. "You're wrong. I'm broken. There is something wrong with me."

"What makes you say this?" She asks as her wings lift her off the ground, carrying her to circle me.

I turn with her as she circles. "I found my mo ghrá geal," I sigh happily. Just thinking of my sweetheart makes my heart beat a little faster. She's stunning. Intelligent eyes, the color of the deepest blue sapphire, immediately drew me in. Perfectly bowed lips begged for my kiss. Silky hair, as black as the darkest winter night, awaited my touch. And her body.

Fuck, that gloriously curvy body was made of pure sin. I have to think about bog slime and the fae who choose to live in that grossness to keep my cock from rising. In countless years of life, I've never reacted this intensely to a woman, and as a Gancanagh, that's been put to the test with a lot of women... and more than a few men.

Gancanagh are natural-born lovers. We love, love. It's not our fault that we fall in love so easily. Or that our mi ghrá geals become enthralled with our seduction and follow us into the fae realm. And it's not as if we don't give their lovers a chance to win them back. They have until midnight on Samhain to woo them back.

Again, not our fault that they historically want nothing to do with their sucky former paramours. When the women, or men, decide to stay, we bring them to the fae realm where they are integrated into our society. We Gancanagh, though, never settle down. Once midnight strikes on Samhain, the lust is broken.

Sometimes, the humans ask to be returned to the human realm when they realize it wasn't real love, and we let them go. We aren't monsters. Most often, they stay and embrace the world of magic.

The idea of letting this woman, whose name I don't even know, go, sends a sharp pain rippling through my body. I have to shake myself to dispel the unpleasantness.

"Your point?" Esmeralda says, landing beside me and folding her delicate arms across her chest. She is rather beautiful for a healing fae. A cascade of blonde curls spills down her back. Her skin has a golden glow to it, almost as if early-morning sunlight is seeping through a silky curtain. Unlike my wings, which match my reflective eyes, hers are a solid snowy white with the slightest pink-rimmed edges. Her face is pretty, all sharp lines with a high brow, thin lips, and knowing green eyes.

But she's not my sweetheart. No one can compare to her beauty.

I shake myself and focus. If I can't fix myself, I'll lose her. That will not be fucking happening.

"When I approached her, she turned me down."

That catches the fae healer's attention. "Elaborate," she demands.

I recite my tale of rejection, explaining how my sweetheart simply thought I was a drunk and confused man.

"Follow me," Esmeralda says before walking briskly down the hallway. I follow her closely, trying to catch the words she's mumbling. After several minutes of twisting and turning through the labyrinth hallways, we arrive at a large wooden door with a tree carved onto it.

"Sit," she commands, waving a hand at a large chair that slides across the room to where I stand. I take a seat as Esmeralda zips around the room, grabbing bottles, herbs, and liquids of various shapes, textures, and colors and depositing them on a long work bench.

She begins to pour this and that into a large bowl, grinding the ingredients with a pestle before adding in some liquid and mixing. I sit quietly for fear of disturbing her and messing up whatever she's doing. This could be what fixes me and allows me to be with my mo ghra geal.

By the time she finally stops grinding, adding, and mixing ingredients, my leg is twitching at a ridiculous rate. I watch as she takes a dropper and extracts what looks like smoke from the bowl. She brings it to her nose and releases the concoction, inhaling it deeply.

Her eyes glow so brightly, I have to turn away, closing mine to shield them from the intensity. When I open them again, Esmeralda stands before me, transformed. Hair wildly flowing in a breeze that isn't there, eyes still eerily bright, and skin radiating light, she looks like the wild fae that once roamed the cliffsides of the Sile before following The Morrigan into the caves.

She takes my hand, turning it over and running a thin finger along the lines of my palm. She repeats the process with the opposite hand before tugging me to stand. Slowly, she traces her finger along my arms and face before circling around me and hovering her hands above my wings.

She walks around me, repeating each process multiple times before exhaling a harsh breath. Her appearance begins to return to normal.

"There's nothing wrong with you, Liam," she says agitatedly.

I slump back down into the chair, my heart sinking to the pits of the nether world.

"At least nothing I can identify. No curse, no hex, no magic inhibiting your natural magic."

"Then why isn't it working?" I cry in despair.

"I'm not sure. Perhaps you need to try again, but use a different approach. Instead of just letting your natural seductive powers lure her in, woo her."

I stare blankly, unsure of what exactly she's trying to say to me.

When the silence stretches, Esmeralda releases an exasperated sigh. "Watch her for a day, maybe two. Figure out how to insert yourself into her life. Get to know her, court her."

"Like the old days," I say, perking up. "How romantic," I sigh.

Esmeralda rolls her eyes.

"Thank you, Esmeralda," I say as I hop up from my chair and stride from the room with purpose.

I need to get back to the human realm so I can observe my mo ghrá geal. The sooner I can figure out how to position myself into her circle, the sooner I can make her mine.

CHAPTER 3

PLOT TWIST
PIPER

"I'm damp."

"It's chilly."

"When are we getting food?"

"Where's the beer?"

"Why are we walking so much?"

I swear to every being in existence, I am going to throttle all three of the idiots on this vacation with me. Maybe I should strangle myself for being dumb enough to bring them. If I hear one more fucking complaint, I am going to lose my ever loving Irish obsessed mind.

One week. We are one week in, and my efforts to live my best Irish adventure life are slowly burning to ashes.

If Curt, Graham, and Cate aren't complaining, they're drinking. And because they're drinking, they're hungover and miserable in the mornings. Which means when they come with me to see the sights and do the tours, all they do is whine and complain. But if I don't drag them with me, they sleep all day, go right back out to the pubs, and get wasted all over again.

By the second time this happened, I was completely over it. Over my so-called boyfriend. Over his best friend and his girlfriend. Over feeling like the fourth wheel on my fucking dream vacation.

Tomorrow, we go to Blarney Castle to kiss the Blarney Stone. It's a complete tourist cliché, but in my Irish-loving heart, my adventure would not be complete without it. My excitement is dimmed though as the Troublesome Trio, as Marie and I have dubbed them, continue to bitch and moan on the train.

"Why is everything spinning?" Cate groans from where she's smashed herself against the train window. Curt lays a sympathetic hand on her knee.

"Not feelin great, hon?" he croaks. Between screaming over the crowds in the pubs when he's wasted and puking his guts out the next morning, Curt sounds like a sickly bullfrog. The sympathy for his hungover friend irks me.

When I told him how sad it made me that he didn't a least come out to see and do the things I had planned, he made it sound like I was the asshole.

"How can you be upset? I don't feel well. I'm not going out when I don't feel well."

"Well, maybe if you didn't get shitfaced with Graham and Cate every night, you wouldn't feel bad. Maybe if you paused for a night, you could come out to do a tour that your girlfriend, who, as a reminder, is the reason you all are here, wants to do. Like boyfriends are supposed to do."

"There's no need to be bitchy, Pippy. We're in a foreign country, I'm going to have a good time."

The second he called me Pippy, I walked out of the hotel room. I loathe being called Pippy. My name is Piper, not fucking Pippy. Now I'm sitting here on the train, wondering how much worse things could get if I go ahead and break up with him here. Because at this point, he feels like an interloper on my vacation, *not* my boyfriend.

Graham peeks his eyes open, glancing at his girlfriend. He's got a beanie pulled down over his close-cut brown hair, bushy eyebrows barely peeking out. I take a minute to give him a once-over.

He and Curt are both athletically built, with wide shoulders, muscled arms, narrow waists, and muscular legs. Graham has brown hair and light hazel eyes, while Curt has sandy blonde hair and dull brown eyes. Neither is bad-looking. But looks only go so far.

Graham turns his eyes to me and tilts his head. "How are you not dying, Pippy?"

I shoot him a glare that could melt icebergs.

"Don't call me Pippy, Graham. You know I hate that. And I'm not dying because I don't get shitfaced nightly." The Troublesome Trio all shoot me dirty looks that I completely ignore.

Whatever he says in response, I don't hear, placing my headphones back on and returning to *Spinning Back to You* by Kat Fallons. The perfect book for my Irish adventure.

Several hours later, we arrive at our hotel for the evening. The trio decides they are all going to lie down, claiming the swaying motion of the train extended their hangovers.

What the fuck ever.

After dropping my bag off in the room, I head downstairs and decide to go for a stroll down Main Street. I'm circling back to the hotel when I get the sense that I'm being watched. It's not the first time this has happened. Over the last few days, wherever I go, I swear someone is watching me. I get a crazy tingling sensation that has goosebumps erupting all over my body.

It's a little unsettling, but my gut tells me that whoever or whatever is watching doesn't mean me any harm. I've been on my own a couple of times at night, too. If whatever it is wanted to hurt me, it has had ample opportunity to do so. Since nothing bad has happened, I've decided that it's a protector, not a threat.

When I get back to the hotel, I head up to the room to see if the Troublesome Trio is recovered enough to grab some dinner. The key card clicks, and I walk into our room, prepared to find Curt either passed out, actively puking, or scrolling his phone. I'm surprised to find an empty room instead.

I hear muffled noise I can't quite place. I follow it to the adjoining room's door, which is cracked open. Pushing it the rest of the way, I freeze in disbelief as I take in the sight before me.

Cate is on her back, moaning like a cat in heat, as Curt pounds into her. At the same time, Graham is grunting like a bull as he fucks Curt's mouth, balls smacking my boyfriends' chin with every hard thrust. And if that isn't enough, I spot all of their phones propped up in different spots, recording. All of them seem oblivious to my invasion of their porn film.

I close the door slowly and softly, grab my suitcase, and head back down to the hotel lobby. At the counter, I inform the clerk that I need to remove the card on file. After confirming with the clerk that they can get new card information from Curt, who is currently in the room, I head out the door and hop into the nearest cab, instructing the driver to take me to a new hotel on the opposite side of the city.

Check-in at my new hotel is easy, thank god, and they are able to give me information to a tour guide's office. Again, I get that feeling of eyes watching, but after what I just saw, I have zero time to dwell on it.

Safe and secure in my room, I call Marie.

"Hey, Boo," she says sleepily.

"Did I wake you?" I ask, guilt gnawing at me.

She yawns, which just makes me feel worse. "You only call

this late or early when something is up. What's going on? Is there a problem with the hotel?"

"No. I'm in a hotel, just not the one I gave you the info for."

"Why?" she asks, tone going on high alert.

I exhale harshly. "Because after we got off the train, we checked into the hotel. The Troublesome Trio said the ride made their hangovers worse and wanted to sleep. I went for a walk and then came back to ask if they wanted food."

My stomach gives a loud rumble. I reach for the room service menu and start browsing. I'm so not going back out. I deserve to indulge after this bullshit.

"Plot twist. I walked in on the making of *Twats Gone Wild*. Curt was fucking Cate, while Graham was fucking Curt's mouth."

I have to hold the phone away from my ear as my bestie screams a long string of profanities. "Don't wake the babies," I chide.

"The babies are fine and not exactly babies. That piece of fucking pond scum. I swear, I'm going to personally remove his ballsack and hang it on the mantle."

I snort-laugh, cause that's an image. "You know, we've been dating for over a year. I should feel something. Sadness, grief, maybe. But all I feel is righteous anger because these mother-fuckers intruded on my fucking dream vacation and made the first week less than enjoyable."

"*That* I am sorry about. That you and dickless are no more, not so much. So what are you gonna do now?"

"I'm at a new hotel, yes, I will text you the info, and I have info for a local travel agent. I'll head over in the morning and make some arrangements. Curt and the others didn't have the itinerary; that was all on me to tell them where we were going and what we were doing. Unless Curt actually listened when I told him what I wanted to do, they won't know where to go.

They will, however, have a lovely surprise in the morning when the clerk knocks on the door to get a good credit card since I removed mine during my exodus."

"That's my girl," Marie says cheerfully. "Go on your adventure. Live your best Irish life. Get laid by a hot guy with a sexy accent and give me the details."

I think of the stranger from my first night here. Thoughts of him have been haunting my dreams. I give a laugh, "Will do, bestie. Love your face."

"Love your face."

We hang up, and I flop back on the bed. First things first, order room service, then look at the remaining things on my to-do list and figure out a plan to bring to the travel agent in the morning.

Even with this cluster fuck, I've got a good feeling. Maybe the luck of the Irish is with me after all.

LET ME BE YOUR GUIDE

LIAM

Something is wrong. Aside from the obvious issues with my magic. No, something is wrong with my mo ghrá geal.

After my visit with Esmerelda, I returned to the human realm and began to observe her and her travel companions. It didn't take long to determine that the companions were utter *scut*. Why my sweetheart would associate with such people is beyond my comprehension. When she is mine, we will surround ourselves with the high fae court and humans that are worthy of her presence.

I've concluded they are on vacation and touring all of Ireland's most popular tourist sites. Where my mo ghrá geal, whose name I have learned is Piper, is excited to visit these sacred locations and learn the histories of my land, the others have no interest. There have been many times I've risked exposure to keep Piper safe when the others abandoned her to get drunk in the local pubs.

Aside from the night we met, Piper hasn't seen me again, yet she can sense me. Those nights when I was close by, watching over her as she roamed the streets soaking in the culture, she'd pause and search the crowd. It was my cloaked presence she sensed, but unlike so many before, she didn't seek me out. No, my fierce Piper walked her own path fearlessly, like a Queen.

Once she's mine, I'll ensure she's treated as the royalty she is. My infatuation with her has only grown as I've watched her. I'm captivated by the way light dances in her eyes when she smiles, the musical note of her laughter, and how her hair has the slightest tint of blue when the sun hits it just right.

I could watch her wander for eternity. The way her hips sway with purpose as she weaves through the crowds to get close to the people reciting long-forgotten histories. I crave to run my hands over her body, mapping out every enticing curve.

I am like any other Gancanagh, I love *love*. Lust is my first language, seduction my second. But these things that I am feeling for Piper are stronger than any I've experienced before. It's terrifying and thrilling.

But last night, something was amiss. I watched Piper re-enter her hotel, then exit with her suitcase and hail a cab to drive her clear across town to a new one. I, of course, followed to ensure her safety. And that's when I got my opening. I overheard her ask the desk clerk about tour guides. Once I heard the name of the agency he suggested, I formed my plan. Now, with a little help from fae magic, I'm sitting behind a desk, awaiting the arrival of my mo ghrá geal.

As if I conjured her from my thoughts, Piper walks through the door, suitcase rolling behind her. She stops short when she spots me, eyes widening in surprise.

"Hello," I say with a smile.

"Hi," she says, sounding a little unsure.

"Welcome to Traditions & Tours. How can I help you?"

She looks around the quiet shop at all the brochures. "I'd like to see about booking a tour guide. I've got a potential plan mapped out and was hoping to see if you offered anything that would fit with what I've got."

"Please take a seat. Let's see what you're looking at."

She walks to the desk and sits, pulling out a folded slip of paper from her cross-body bag. I take a moment to appreciate the way the strap lies perfectly between the valley of her generous tits and use her momentary distraction as she gets settled to adjust my rapidly rising cock under the desk.

Even in a simple sweater and leggings with her hair pulled into a low pony, she is a vision. She unfolds the paper and hands it to me.

I study the locations and use all my self-control to contain my elation. In addition to the typical tourist spots, Piper wants to see the home of real magic and legend. The Hell Caves, the Hill of Tara, and she wants to finish her trip with the celebration of Samhain in Derry.

It's perfect. It's fate.

I set the paper down and give her my best charming smile. "Hunting for fairies, Ms—?"

"Oh, I'm so sorry," she exclaims, reaching her hand over the desk, completely unfazed by my fae charm. "I'm Piper, Piper Harris. And definitely."

The moment our hands connect, my vision goes blurry, my blood heats, and my already hard cock nearly erupts. It's such a strong reaction, I nearly forget to introduce myself.

"Lovely to meet you, Ms. Harris. I'm Liam Sullivan," I say dazedly.

"Piper, please," she says, a little breathless.

"Piper," I say on a sigh.

We stare at each other for a moment before she gives me an unsure smile. "Do you remember me? From the pub the other night?"

I do my best to look bashful before replying, "Ah, I was

hoping you wouldn't remember. I must apologize, I was a little out of sorts. It would seem that fate is giving me a chance to make it up to you."

"Oh, no need to make it up to me. No harm done. I'm just glad to see you're alright."

I release my pheromones to test their effectiveness. Now that I've felt her silky touch, the need to make her mine has increased exponentially. Perhaps the other night was a fluke.

"So what can we do about my tour? Will we need to coordinate with other agencies? Do I need to mark things off?" She asks, still apparently immune to my magic.

Buggar. I am most definitely fucking broken. My seductive nature, my pheromones, nothing is fucking working on her. Me, on the other hand... Her glorious scent is making me harder than steel.

I try to relax my tense body. Why the fuck does my magic not work on her. Why do I react to her so intensely?

What. The. Actual. Fuck.

Clearing my throat, I reply, "Oh no, we can fit all of this in before the festival in Derry. No promises on the fairies, though. They are precarious beings. If they want to be seen, they'll show themselves to you." I wink.

"And no need for other agencies. As it so happens, my schedule is completely open. We can kick things off today at Blarney Castle. I'll just need to write up the paperwork and make a few arrangements."

All of those things will be taken care of magically, of course. Paperwork is the fucking worst.

Piper makes a little *O* with her mouth. Images of my cock sliding in out of that wet heat bombard me, and I just barely stifle a groan.

"Really?" she asks.

"Hand to the Blarney Stone," I say with a cocky smile.

She laughs, the sound resonating deep inside of me. Warmth spreads throughout my body as I soak in the sound and the smile that accompanies it.

"Let's do it!" she says excitedly.

A few hours later, arrangements magically made, magical paperwork signed, payment received—and returned, unbeknownst to Piper—we are on our way to Blarney Castle.

En route, Piper receives a phone call from one of her traveling companions, who seems quite upset. I can't suppress my chuckle when she tells him to fuck off and hangs up on him.

She catches my snicker and gives me a small smile, but her eyes don't sparkle the way they did when I told her I could take her on her dream vacation. I want to ask what's wrong, but I decide to focus on easing her into relaxing in my presence.

The need to touch her is overwhelming. It takes effort not to hold her hand as we walk the castle grounds. Since my magic doesn't affect her, I'll have to win her over the old-fashioned way, and that does not include groping a woman I barely know.

Step one of my plan, observe my mo ghrá geal and enter her life, is complete. Now for step two: seduce her by wooing her like a princess in a fairytale. Then on to step three: keep her until midnight on Samhain.

The question, one that no self-respecting Gancanagh should ever have, is, what if I don't want to let her go?

CHAPTER 5

GRAND IRISH ADVENTURE

PIPER

"You seriously tried to carve a turnip?" Liam asks with an amused smirk.

I nod enthusiastically, flipping my phone around to show him the picture of my monstrous attempt at an authentic Irish Jack-O-Lantern.

Liam takes the phone from me and snorts. "That is truly terrible, Pip. Seriously, this could be a prop in a horror movie."

"You're not wrong, but I was trying to be authentic, damn it. It's not my fault I've got the crafting talents of a toddler."

We both burst out laughing, only stopping when my phone rings. Liam hands me the phone, wiping tears from his eyes.

The number is unknown, but the country code tells me it's local. I'm positive I already know who it is, but I answer just in case it's one of the hotels or rental agencies. Everything Liam arranged for us is under my name, and I don't want to risk a delay by not answering.

"Hello," I answer hesitantly. Liam gives me a concerned look from where he sits across from me in our train car. It's the same look he's given me each time the phone has rung and I've answered since we started our grand Irish adventure.

"What the fuck Piper! Are you seriously going to make me chase you all over this stupid ass country? I-"

I don't let Curt finish his tirade. As soon as I hang up, I block yet another number and toss the phone on the seat next to me.

"Are you alright, Piper?" Liam's soft, accented voice asks.

I give him the most genuine smile I can manage. "I'm fine. He's not."

We're quiet for a moment, the motion of the train rocking us gently, the sounds a pleasant background noise to our journey.

And what an amazing journey it's been so far.

Hiring Liam was the best decision I've made since landing. Our first stop was Blarney. We had an incredible lunch at Muskerry Arms before heading up to Blarney Castle. I got to walk around the stunning grounds and explore the poison garden. I wandered around for I don't even know how long, stopping to take pictures of the many varieties of flowers and asking questions about them.

Liam never complained. Never whined or told me he was bored. He answered every question and encouraged me to explore to my heart's content. He even managed to find a fairy crown made of flowers in the gardens. Where he got it from, I couldn't say. When I asked him, he simply said "Fairy magic" and gave me a wink and a mischievous smile.

When he presented it to me, he bowed low like we were in a grand palace and not a garden. He placed the crown on my head and called me *Mo Bhanrion,* my queen.

The look he gave me then could make a statue blush with its intensity. When I looked into his eyes, I saw a lusty inferno, but under the blaze, there was something else I couldn't quite define. It did nothing to quell my growing attraction to him, which was absolutely absurd, since we'd met mere hours before.

When I reluctantly finished in the gardens, we headed up the narrow stairs to the famous Blarney Stone.

Liam got some great pictures of me kissing the stone before I strong-armed him into kissing it himself. It was the best day I'd had since I arrived, and that wasn't even the best part.

At sunset, Liam took me back to the eastern side of the Castle to Rock Close, the home of an ancient Druid settlement. We walked with oil lanterns through trees to the sacrificial altar, then to the witches' kitchen.

"Can you feel the magic in the air?" Liam whispered near my ear while we were near the witches' kitchen.

Shivers had run up my spine. I could feel the magic. It was in the air and the ground all around us. I swear, for a brief moment, when I looked at Liam, I could see wings on his back and tiny horns in his hair.

I'd blinked, and Liam was, well, Liam. No wings, no horns. Just Liam in his sweater, jeans, and peacoat. He'd given me a mischievous smile and offered me his arm. We walked arm in arm through the forest and the castle grounds until the witching hour, talking about everything from magic to my job as a graphic designer.

The visit to the Hell Caves had been the same. Magic swirled all around me as Liam and I explored the cave. Liam held my hand to keep me steady, holding on just a moment longer than necessary before letting go.

One odd thing had happened, though. A little girl kept pointing at him and telling her mother to look at the fairy. When I turned to look at him, his appearance seemed different. His skin had taken on a grayish hue, his eyes were a kaleido-scope of colors, and he had stunning wings the same shade as his eyes with red tips. I'd blinked, and it was all gone.

"It's the ears," he teased, referring to his long and slightly pointed ears, as he took my hand to help me through the tunnel.

If I weren't aware of the fact that I was literally paying him to be my guide, I'd say this was the best string of dates I've ever been on. The more time I spend with him, the more I like him. Which is problematic, since this trip has an expiration date. But I can't deny the chemistry between us. The easy conversation. The banter. The incredibly hot wet dreams that have me waking up panting and soaked.

The thought of the end of my adventure causes a painful ache in my heart.

Marie keeps telling me to live my best Irish adventure life and jump Liam's bones. She saw him on video chat and immediately said, "Hit that for both of us." If Liam heard her, he was too gentlemanly to say, but he did have more swagger after that particular call.

"Piper," Liam says, taking my hand and pulling me from my thoughts.

"I left him," I say, looking out the window and letting the warmth and now familiar comfort of Liam's hand soothe me. "Them," I correct. This is the one subject we haven't discussed, even though I know he's heard the screams from the other end of the line.

"Who?"

"My boyfriend, well, *ex*-boyfriend, his best friend, and his best friend's girlfriend. The people who crashed my vacation. I've been planning this vacation for years. When I was finally ready, I invited my boyfriend. Then, all of the sudden, his bestie and his bestie's girlfriend are going too. That's not the problem. You know what, no. It's *part* of the problem. I don't like them. They crashed my vacation, bitched about every possible thing, and then had the fucking nerve to make a ménage à trois porno in the hotel room while I was out for a walk."

I look at Liam, who looks like he's ready to murder my ex

and his friends. His eyes shift to something dark and stormy, like an angry ocean.

"Bastards are unworthy of your company, croís milis." The storm in his eyes passes, replaced by a tender softness. "But their loss is my gain," he states before gently lifting my hand to brush his lips across my knuckles.

Goosebumps erupt all over my body, and heat courses through me. It's the same visceral reaction every time we touch. My body lights up with need and desire and longing. The last few days with Liam have felt...incredible. Like we fit even though we're strangers. When I think of him, my heart beats fast and flights of fairies erupt inside of me. It's the kind of feeling you feel when you're falling in love. Which is ridiculous, since we just met.

The train comes to a stop, and the conductor announces our arrival at Roscommon. The moment is broken, our hands releasing to gather our belongings. From the train station, we rent a car and head to our hotel in Navan. Halloween decorations are scattered about the town. Ghosts hang in trees, jack-o-lanterns sit on porches, and witches' hats adorn fence lines. I soak in every single thing.

Liam assures me we have plenty of time before we need to leave for the Hill of Tara. I'm beyond excited for this particular stop on my adventure. In addition to being the High seat of the kings and Queens of Ireland, it's also the mythological home to the fairies. I'm hoping to catch a glimpse of the fairies, even if it's only for a moment.

Since we have time, I jump in the shower for a refresh. Well, a refresh and a slightly cuter outfit. If I'm going to meet a fairy, I need to look my best. Yup, that's what I'm going with. Nothing to do with the hot tour guide whose touch heats my blood and accent soaks my panties.

"Piper," Liam's voice accompanies a light knock on the door. "Are you ready for our next adventure?"

CHAPTER 6
KISS ME I'M IRISH
LIAM

Every night when we retire for the evening, I head to my room to relive the memories of every smile, every touch, and every stolen glance from the day while I fuck my hand to the scent of Piper that clings to me. There's no satisfaction in it, but if I don't get some relief, I'll go feral from need and the longing to be inside of her.

But it's no longer just lust and sexual need. I want *her*. Her company. Her laugh. The smile that makes her eyes sparkle. The way she becomes animated when she tells a story. All of it. And I don't know how to deal with this. Never have I had these longings before.

Which is why after I temporarily take the edge off of my aching cock, I transport myself back to the fairy realm to have Esmerelda examine me again. Just to check in for the sake of my sanity.

Not that it's doing any good.

"I'm still broken," I groan as her eyes return to their normal shade.

She heaves a sigh, just like she's done every night for nearly a week, and rolls her eyes.

"I still find nothing wrong with you. Because, despite what you keep saying, you are not broken."

"Or you're defective," I snap.

I realize my mistake as her eyes flare to an icy white. A frigid wind sweeps through the room as magic crackles in the air. Esmeralda circles me in a flash, ice trailing in her wake and covering the chair beneath me.

"Apologies," I yell over the gust. "I'm just frustrated."

Her eyes narrow but slowly fade as she stops and steps back. The ice melts to a puddle beneath my chair, and the wind disappears.

"How did you do that?" I ask, slightly dazed and confused.

"My mother is an ice fae, my father a healer. I am the best of both," she says matter-of-factly. "I understand you're frustrated, Liam, but there is nothing wrong with you or your magic."

I slump back in the chair and pout.

"She's unaffected by my magic. I keep amping up my magical charm, releasing my pheromones, and I get nothing. How can I hope to seduce her into being mine by Halloween if my magic is useless? I don't know what to do."

If Esmerelda told me to slather myself with honey, roll through a field of thistles, and kiss a pig before dancing naked in a circle backwards...I'd do it with a smile on my face to entice Piper to be mine. I'm desperate.

Every moment I spend with her, I want her more. I love the way she smiles as I tell stories of the fae or the history of my homeland. The look of wonder on her face each time we explore a new location will forever be one of my favorite expressions. I love how happy it makes her to just walk and talk with me, even if it's about nothing but the weather. And the way my heart races every time we touch. I crave that feeling. I crave all of it, crave her.

I don't realize how lost in my thoughts I am until Esmerelda clears her throat.

"Huh?" I ask.

"I said she's unaffected by your magic, but is she unaffected by you?"

"How do you mean?" I ask her. The magic and I are one and the same.

"You're wooing her, aren't you?"

"Yes."

"So stop thinking of the magic and tell me if she responds to *you*."

I think about her question. Every time I've tried to use magic on Piper, I've gotten no response. But... But when we are together, strolling the forest or walking through the village, it's different. She smiles and laughs with me. Takes my arm or lets me hold her hand, and leans into my touch.

"She does. When I'm not trying, she's relaxed and responsive to my touch, even though I don't mean it as seductive. And she reaches for me. Just simple touches like placing her head on my shoulder in the cab on the ride to the hotel or threading her arm through mine when we walk in the village."

Esmerelda nods enthusiastically. "So she's immune to your magic but not to you. Interesting."

"Interesting how?"

She bats away my question with a wave of her hand, sitting up a little straighter now, observing me.

"How do you feel right now? When you're here and she's there?"

I think for a moment before answering, "I miss her. Like I left part of myself with her when I came here."

Esmerelda nods again and points to me. "Every time you've come here, save the night you met her, you've sat in that chair moaning about your allegedly broken magic, all while rubbing your chest."

I look down and see she's right. I am rubbing small circles on my chest above my heart.

"And when you think of her, how do you feel?"

"Like I'm in love," I automatically answer.

"Interesting."

"What?" I asked, alarmed.

She shrugs a shoulder. "How does that compare to your past mo ghrá geals?"

"There is no comparison," I snap. Why she would ask such a thing is beyond me.

A slow smile spreads across her face. "Elaborate."

Still glaring at her, I explain my feelings. "I want her. Not just physically, although I feel like if I can't have her that way, I may perish from blue balls," I grumble, crossing my arms defensively. "I want *her*, period. I crave her company and her smile, and I hate being apart from her."

"Do you now? I think I may know what's going on here."

"What?" I say, jumping to my feet.

She leans back in her chair, nonchalantly draping her wings like a cape. "I think you've found your anam cara."

Magic seizes me with such force that my knees give out, and I crash to the floor, head spinning. Esmerelda rushes to my side and helps me into the chair.

"Are you alright?" she asks as she checks me over.

"No, I think I'm in shock. The moment you said the words, they resonated in my heart and sent shockwaves through my magic. My soulmate, Esmerelda. Is it really possible?"

"It's rare, but it is the one explanation that makes sense. Your magic has no effect on her. She's immune to your enchanted charms, but not to you. You miss her and can't even bring yourself to brag over your past conquests. It fits."

"I have a soulmate," I murmur in awe with a love-sick smile...that immediately drops. "And she's leaving. After Samhain, she'll travel back to her home."

Esmerelda gives me a sympathetic look. "Then you have a choice to make. Win her or let her go."

I manage to stand and straighten my spine. "There is no choice," I say before marching from the hall and transporting myself back to the human realm. I have a plan, I just pray the luck of my people is on my side.

PIPER HAS BEEN SO EXCITED ABOUT THE HILL OF TARA, I WANT TO make it extra special for her. With the revelation that she is my soulmate, not just my mo ghrá geal, not just my annual Samhain conquest, I need to up my game. While she settles into the hotel, I contact a few friends to arrange something special for our visit.

"Are you ready for our next adventure?" I ask as I knock on Piper's door.

The door swings open, and I have to clench my jaw to keep my mouth from hanging open like a cartoon. She's changed out of the leggings and hoodie she had on for the trip from Owey-nagat. Now, she wears jeans that mold to her body, accentuating each and every curve, and a snug sweater with a deep V that gives me a glimpse of the swell of her breasts.

My hands flex and release to keep from dragging her body flush with mine and crashing our mouths together. As I stand there, dumbstruck, Piper gives me a sassy smile.

"Is this acceptable fairy hunting attire? I was going to go with my *Kiss me I'm Irish* shirt, but thought better of it," she says, doing a little spin before stepping out of the way for me to come in.

I swallow hard before speaking. "You run the risk of being taken," I rasp, thinking of the many ways I'd like to take her.

"As long as it's a nice fae that takes me, I won't complain."

Minx. I move the basket I've had stashed behind my back in front of my rapidly rising cock.

Piper gives an excited hop. "Is that a picnic basket?" She asks excitedly.

I nod my head, my smile stretching wide at her delight. "I thought we might have a sunset picnic before we go looking for fairies on the hill."

She lets out a shriek of delight before throwing her arms around my neck. I move the basket to the side so I can pull her close.

Fucking hell, I've been dying to hold her like this for days. Her body molds perfectly to mine, and for a moment, I lose myself to the feeling of our bodies pressed tight, imagining what it would feel like with no clothing between us.

"I love picnics," she says happily, as I breathe deeply of her sweet and floral scent. I reluctantly release her before my cock starts jabbing her.

When our eyes meet, there's something there that I haven't seen before. A subtle shift, as if she's come to a realization. Her smile is dazzling as she turns out of my arms to walk towards the bed.

"Let me get my coat and scarf, and we can go."

Her happiness wraps around me like my wings, familiar and comforting. I want to make her happy, to feel her joy every day. Once her coat is on, I offer her my arm, and we're off on our next adventure.

"WHAT WOULD YOU DO IF YOU SAW A REAL FAIRY?" I ASK AS WE EAT our picnic dessert. Every moment I've had with Piper has been my favorite, but this little picnic may just be the best of the best. We've laughed so hard we've cried while talking about everything and nothing and enjoying the simple meal I prepared for us.

We arrived at the Hill of Tara about an hour before the sun began to set. I've been to this place of reverence countless times over my lifetime, and it still resonates within me. The power here is like no other, steeped with deep magic passed from the Tuatha Dé Danann. The castles of old have long since been reclaimed by the Earth, but what remains still draws droves of people daily.

I wanted Piper to experience this place in its natural state, without the crowds. The way that I see and feel it. We walked the loop arm in arm, Piper hanging on every word as I told her the rich histories of the hill, both human and fairy. The chief perk of having magic is being able to use it in moments like this. While we've explored under the light of the moon, we've been cloaked in magic so no one could detect us.

Once we completed the loop and the sun had dropped below the horizon, I set up our picnic. I spread a large blanket on the ground and laid another to the side, knowing we'd need it for a wrap once the temperature dropped. Carefully, I lit the oil lamps and laid out our meal of Irish soda bread, stew, and apple cake.

Now, Piper sits next to me under our shared blanket, legs outstretched, eating the remnants of her apple cake. "I'd watch as long as they'd let me, then I'd have the most incredible memory."

"You wouldn't question it?" I ask her as I finish off my own slice.

"Nope. I've always believed there are things in the world I can't see, either because they don't want me to see them or because I'm not ready to see them yet," she says with a dreamy expression. "What?" she asks when she looks back at me.

"You are a rare gem, Piper. Not many people would be so open-minded."

"What about you? What would you do if you saw a fairy?"

I give her a sly smile. "Oh, I'd ask to join in whatever adventure they were off to have." Piper laughs and shakes her head. "And on that note. Why don't we pack this up and drop it off at the car, then go see if we can find some fairies."

"Let's do it."

Once the picnic is packed up and in the car, we take the lanterns and travel back to the hill to the Lia Fail, the coronation stone. We cast our lantern glow here and there, looking for the fairies who haunt this place. Piper's special surprise should be coming up any moment now.

As we near the stone, Piper pauses. "Did you hear that?" she whispers.

"Hear want, Cailín?" I ask, hiding my smile in the shadows.

She turns in a circle, looking past the glow of the lamps to the darkness. "I thought I heard something." She starts walking again, cautiously, yet there's excitement buzzing off of her.

A few moments later, I pause. "Piper," I whisper. "I heard something."

"Me too," she whispers, turning to me with a smile. "Let's keep going."

We walk just a bit further, and Piper grabs my arm, then points ahead. We've finally stumbled upon my surprise.

All around Lia Fail, fairies dance and fly to a merry tune around fires lit around the stone.

"Fairies," Piper mouths, grabbing my hand and creeping closer. She stops as close as she dares and dims the lanterns. We sit side by side, hand in hand, as my friends continue to dance merrily. The absolute awe on her face cracks something wide open in my chest. Pure joy radiates from her as unshed tears sparkle in her eyes.

I lean over and whisper in her ear, "Do you want to take a picture or video?"

She shakes her head, wiping her eyes with her free hand. "No. This was meant for us to see, not for us to share. I'll remember this as vividly in fifty years as I do right now," she whispers back.

My heart swells. She would keep the secrets of my people to protect them. When I asked my friends to put on this show for Piper, I had every intention of making this night special for her. It turns out, I made it special for us both.

Soon the firelight fades, the music stops, and the fairies take their leave. We sit in the quiet long after they've gone, soaking in the magic of the night. Piper shivers, and I know it's time to go. I rise, pulling her with me, and lead us back to the car.

The drive back to our hotel is filled with companionable silence.

"Thank you," Piper says when we stand outside of our hotel rooms. "Thank you for the most magical night of my life."

I brush a finger down her cheek. "It was my pleasure," I say softly. She takes my hand and pulls me to her, into a passionate kiss.

CHAPTER 7

FAIRY WINGS & SECRET THINGS

PIPER

Liam's lips are firm and sure against mine. He tastes like my favorite spiced apple wine, dark and alluring with a hint of spice. I'm instantly addicted.

Which is an immediate problem. I shove the intrusive thoughts of my impending departure away and focus on the here and now.

Liam slides his hand up my cheek and tilts my head to deepen our kiss, dropping the picnic basket to the ground. My lips part for him as he sweeps his tongue along their seam. His tongue slips into my mouth, tangling with mine as he walks me backwards to press me against my hotel room door.

Pleasure like I've never felt pulses through my body as our kiss becomes more desperate and heated. His other hand coils around my waist, pressing us closer, molding our bodies together, and ensuring there's no part of us that doesn't touch.

His hand slips beneath my sweater, skimming my ribs before cupping one of my generous breasts. A throaty moan escapes me as his thumb brushes my nipple, which pebbles beneath his ministration. My hands find their way to his waist, lifting up the heavy sweater he wears to touch his bare skin.

Electricity ripples through my body as my fingertips trace the hard muscles of his abs. His cock jerks against me, a slow pulse I can feel in spite of the layers of clothing between us.

When we break apart, both desperate for air, Liam presses his forehead to mine.

'Better than my dreams," he whispers before sweeping a chaste kiss on my lips.

He dreams of me just like I dream of him. The knowledge evaporates whatever hesitation I have left.

"Liam," I say breathlessly, looking deep into eyes that can't seem to settle on a color. The air is charged; whether it's from our encounter with the fairies or the magic of the veil between worlds thinning so close to Halloween, I don't know. Or it could be just us. Whatever the reason, magic is all around us.

He cups my face with both hands and searches my eyes. "Are you sure?" he asks, his voice laced with concern.

I dig in my pocket and retrieve the room key, pressing it to the lock until it clicks. I use one hand to turn the handle and the other to drag Liam into the room.

Once we're inside, I back him into the door. "Positive," I say before claiming his lips again. He wastes no time pushing my jacket off my shoulders as I kick my shoes off. I do the same to him, pushing the heavy jacket off his muscled shoulders to join mine on the ground.

Strong hands cup my ass and lift me, and my legs wrap naturally around his waist as he walks from the door to the bed. I trail kisses along his jaw, nipping his ear, then kissing his neck.

"Fuck mo chroi, I want to take my time. Worship this body the way it was made for, but I have to have you."

Well fuck me sideways. Wetness gushes from my pussy, effectively ruining my panties. I have never felt so empowered, sexy, and wanted by a man. The way Liam looks at me, like I am not only the only woman in the world but also the very center of his universe, makes my pulse race. His words strike a chord within, harmonizing with my identical feelings for him.

He sets me down on the bed, and I grab the hem of his sweater and pull it over his head. Whatever I imagined as my fingertips traced his muscles moments ago pales in comparison to the chiseled work of art before me.

He's well defined, toned and taut, a hotter-than-sin work of art I want to lick like a lollipop.

Before I can reach for his belt and pants, my arms are lifted, and my sweater and bra are pulled off my body in one fluid motion. My heavy breasts fall free, bouncing and swinging as gravity claims them.

My first instinct is to cover them, my second, to desperately reach for the bedside lamp to turn off the light. Curt was never a fan of my breasts, always complaining they were too big and that I should get a reduction. The thought comes and goes like lightning as Liam leans down and sucks one sensitive bud into his mouth while kneading the other.

My back arches into Liam's touch as he switches his hands and mouth.

"Gloriously fucking perfect. Such perfect tits," He says, lightly nipping one bud then the other, cupping them in his large hands. "Look at how beautiful they look spilling over my hands, mo chroí."

All I can do is moan and nod my head. He releases my breasts and gently pushes my shoulders so I lie down on the bed, then removes the rest of my clothing. Once I'm fully naked, he stands and stares.

I swear I can see subtle shifts in his face; his ears are more pointed, his face a tad more angular. And are those wings that seem to flash in and out of focus?

"Stunning," he murmurs while unbuckling his pants, undoing his zipper, and pushing them to the ground. He cock springs free, not overly long, but thick and veined. Generous amounts of precum leak steadily from the wide tip. I want to run my tongue over him, ending at his cock to lick every drop.

Liam crawls onto the bed, lifting one leg and kissing from my ankle up my calf until he reaches my dripping core. He buries his face between my legs and dives into my pussy without pretense or warning.

I gasp as his tongue plunders my lower lips, licking and sucking like a starved animal. My legs wrap around his head as he continues to pleasure me with his mouth. Two fingers slip inside me as he sucks my clit into his mouth. The orgasm hits me fast and hard, my thighs squeezing his head.

He licks me until the spasms subside, and my legs fall like lead to the sides. When he lifts his head, there's a wicked gleam in his eyes and a devilish grin on his face as he licks his lips.

"Delicious," he practically growls, crawling up my body. He kisses me passionately as his cock slides into my channel, the thickness stretching me open for him.

"Liam," I moan when he withdraws and slides back in. "You feel so good. So thick," I ramble as pleasure wracks my body.

"Mmm," he hums against my throat. "You feel like paradise, mo chroí. This body was made for me to pleasure. Your pussy was made for my cock." He kisses the tender flesh of my neck, sucking there as he begins to move with purpose.

As his tempo increases, he cups my breasts, toying with my hard nipples before leaning down to suck one then the other.

"So beautiful," he pants, "You're so beautiful, Piper."

He adjusts his position over me, lifting my hips to drive his cock in deeper and drawing sounds from me I've never heard before. When I look up at him, the air around him shimmers. His eyes become iridescent, a kaleidoscope of colors. His ears are completely pointed, two small horns peek out of his hairline, and a pair of incredible wings flutter behind his back.

"You're a fairy," I manage to pant as I feel my inner walls begin to flutter.

"Yes. What you see is real. Piper. What you feel is real. Does what I am change that?" he asks, never losing his pace, then leans down to kiss me once more.

"No," I say with absolute certainty when he releases my lips.

"Good," he growls, kissing along my jawline to my ear. "Now scream my name when you come, mo chroi." With that, his pistons into me while reaching between us to pinch my clit.

I scream his name as the most intense orgasm of my life hits me, stealing my sight as stars dance before my eyes. Moments later, Liam cries out my name as his hot cum fills me. When his orgasm passes, he leans down and kisses me softly before rolling us so I'm lying on his chest. Once we're situated, he drapes his wings gently around me.

I look up and study him, finding him doing the same to me.

"Are you alright?" he asks hesitantly.

"Am I dreaming?" I ask.

"No," he replies tightly.

"Coma?" I question.

"No."

"Brain damage, stroke, or mental break?" I ask with a smirk.

"Definitely not," he replies.

"Then I'm perfect." I sigh contentedly, resting my cheek on his firm chest.

His wings give a little flutter against my skin as his hands start to rub up and down my sides.

"You're taking this remarkably well," he comments in an amused tone.

I look up to his stunning eyes and smile. "I told you. I believe in things I can't see. Fairy wings and secret things and all manner of other things are out there that humans have no clue about. I'm happy you showed yourself to me. Although I have to confess, I think I saw glimpses of you a few times on this adventure of ours."

"I wondered, but thought I played it off well," He says with that mischievous smile I love.

Love. Oh fuck, I think I do actually love him. And that's crazy. This is probably just a fling for him, no matter how convincing his words were.

Halloween is only a few days away, and with the end of Halloween comes the end of my grand Irish adventure. My heart soars as he pulls me up to kiss me once more, then plummets.

What am I going to do now?

CHAPTER 8

IT'S NOT LIKE THAT NOW

LIAM

Piper moans as I suck one of her rosy nipples into my mouth. She must be exhausted from the marathon sex we've been having, but I can't get enough of her, and she can't seem to get enough of me.

"You're insatiable," she mumbles sleepily, raking her fingers through my hair, grazing my horns with her thumbs, and pressing me closer.

"You're addictive," I counter when I release the now tight bud only to suck the other into my mouth. Piper's giggle turns into a raspy moan. Gods, I do love the pleasurable noises I draw from her.

After our first night together, which I catalog as the best night of my fucking life, I made love to her several more times until the sun rose, drawing every possible ounce of pleasure from her body before exhaustion took her.

We spent the next day back at the Hill of Tara so Piper could explore the ruins in the light of day. I explained how I had arranged for some of my friends to come and put on a show for her, ensuring her experience was the most magical possible.

The beautiful smile that lit up her face made my heart skip a beat. When she kissed me, I felt her soul reaching for mine as joy radiated from within her. What had begun as a sweet and grateful kiss quickly began to morph into something deep and needy. Piper decided she was through exploring the hill in favor of exploring my body in her hotel room for the remainder of the day and well into the night.

We arrived in Derry yesterday and spent the day wandering the town and taking in the exquisite decorations for the festival. We listened to tales and haunted histories while we ate our lunch and tried our hands at carving pumpkins. Piper, clearly an expert, carved a moon and cat into hers with ease. It wasn't until I used my magic, something that Piper now can sense, that I was able to carve the simple ghost in my own pumpkin.

When evening fell, we went on a haunted tour that concluded with a beautiful fireworks display. After a small dinner, we danced in the street to a local band playing everything from upbeat jigs to the traditional Irish Waltz. I held her close and savored each moment, praying that when midnight struck on Samhain, she'd still be mine.

Our connection has steadily grown since we've become intimate, yet I could sense a growing distance as well. I'd noticed a sadness in her eyes sometimes when she looked away from me or thought I wasn't looking.

Her ex has called once since we arrived, but that call was like all the others. She hung up on him and blocked the number immediately. Still, I wonder if that's what troubles her or if it's the ticking clock that I hear as each day ends.

The thought of losing her steals my breath and stabs my heart. This must be what love feels like. Real love. Not the lustful magic of the Gancanagh but true love. Living without her is unthinkable, but how can I convince her to stay?

Piper's moan draws me from my thoughts and returns me to the present.

"I'm not the one with the magically addictive tongue."

I give a dark chuckle as I position myself between her legs. "I beg to differ, mo chroi. Your mouth is the most wickedly delicious kind of magic."

My cock slides in to the hilt, drawing a satisfied moan from both of us. In moments, we're both lost to the pleasure of our joined bodies. I roll onto my back, wings splayed out over the sides of the bed to let Piper ride me.

She rises up and slams home, leaning back at a new angle. Pleasure zip up my spin as I grip her hips and help her move. Her fingertips slide down my legs and brush my sensitive wings. I jerk my hips up as I'm nearly blinded by rapture.

"Fuck, Piper, touch them again."

She does as I ask and runs her fingers along the sensitive skin of my wings. I grip her hips tightly and slam her up and down at a rhythm that would make most humans pass out. Not my Piper, she wraps her hands around my to steady herself and lets me control her body as her tits bounce wildly.

She throws her head back, lost to her own pleasure, and chants my name as she cums, squirting her elixir all over my cock.

"Piper!" I bellow to the ceiling as I arch my back and ram home one last time. Every time I cum inside her, I think it's the most incredible orgasm of my life, and yet every time I do it again, it only gets better.

I pull her down to me and kiss her, pouring all the love I feel for her into the kiss and praying she feels it—that she feels the same.

"You are by far the best way to wake up in the morning," she says breathily.

"I'd argue that it's more like noon, and you are far better than I, but I don't know that you'd let me win that argument." I'm gifted a sweet smile and a quick peck on the lips before she rolls off of me. Instantly, I want to pull her back into my arms. I loathe being apart from her.

"We should probably shower and get something to eat. I'd love to do a little shopping today if you don't mind. Then we could drop everything off and get dinner before the festival starts. "

"Don't mind at all," I say, stretching. When I sit up, I catch her sad expression in the mirror, and my heart clenches. I can't lose her. Tonight, I'll tell her how I feel, and we can figure things out together. I don't care if she doesn't want to stay here. I'll go wherever she goes.

An hour later, we are walking down one of the packed streets, browsing the goods and wares of the many artisans attending the festival. Piper has already made several purchases. I've got a bag full of honey and jam as well as a large bag stuffed with a crochet blanket for her best friend.

We've just stopped at the stall of a lovely young man selling wool scarves when I'm overcome with a sense of danger and foreboding.

"Piper!"

The voice is strident, angry, and familiar. With a start, I realize it's the same voice I've heard shouting through Piper's phone.

She turns in the direction of her name, eyes going wide.

"Curt?" she asks, confused.

Curt, her fuckwad ex, marches over to the stall and attempts to loom in front of her. I immediately step between them, taking a protective stance.

"Get the fuck out of my way. I need to have a word with my girlfriend."

"Ex-girlfriend," she corrects while stepping out from behind me.

"You need to back up, gobshite, and adjust your fucking

tone. That is no way to speak to a lady." I can feel magic building, aching to turn this eejit into pond scum.

Curt leers at me as he shoves past to get to Piper. "Fuck you, asshole."

"What the fuck, Piper? You just fucking disappeared and left me to pay the fucking hotel bill! Do you know how hard it was to fucking find you?"

"It wouldn't have been hard if you'd actually given a shit about this trip. And I wouldn't have disappeared if I hadn't walked in on you fucking Cate and blowing Graham at the same time!"

To his credit, Curt takes a startled step back.

"Oh yeah. I saw your little porno, phones propped up to film. There was no way in fucking hell I was footing the bill for the three of you to get your fucking freak on and ruin my dream vacation." She hisses at him.

My chest puffs up with pride as Piper plants her feet and places her hands on her hips, daring him to try and talk his way out the shit hole he's dug for himself.

He sputters a moment, then reaches out and lays a hand on her arm. "We were drunk, baby. It was all a drunken mistake. Let's go somewhere and talk. Take in the festival. Make the best of the end of our trip."

I damn near rip the fuckers arm from its socket.

"Don't you fucking lay a hand on her. You'll have your chance to win her back just before midnight. Until then, stay the fuck away."

"Fuck you, jackass," he says, pushing away from me. "I'll be at the festival, Piper. Come find me when you lose the dickhead." He flips me off as he walks away.

My chest is heaving, and my heart is pounding in my ears. I'm ready to destroy Piper's ex. She lays a hand on me, and my rage calms, but it is quickly replaced by worry when I look at Piper.

"What did you mean? Just now, when you told him he'd have a chance to win me back?"

"Piper," I say, taking her hand and leading her to a side alley so we can speak.

She looks at me with such vulnerability, it breaks my heart wide open. "This has to do with the fact that you're fae."

"I'm a Gancanagh, a love talker." Piper drops my hand and wraps her arms around herself.

"You seduce people away from the ones they love. Lure them to the fairy realm. Their loved ones have until midnight of Halloween to win them back, or they're lost to the fae realm. I know the legend. None of this is real. The way I feel about you, it's all magic," she says sadly.

"Piper, Mo chroi. No. No, what you feel is real. What I feel is real. Yes, it started that way. My magic, it drew me to you. It's not like that now.

I saw you across the pub and knew you had to be mine. But then, my magic didn't work on you. Not my charms, or my enchanted flowers, or the pheromones I release. Nothing affected you. "

"Your magic doesn't work on me," she says skeptically.

"It doesn't, mo chroi. I swear. Everything we've shared has been real. I love you, Piper. I love you," I plead, ready to drop to my knees.

"I-I need to go," she says, whirling around and running into the crowd.

CHAPTER 9

SO LONG, SAMHAIN

PIPER

He's a fae; of course it wasn't real. I'm such a fool, I think as I wander through the crowded festival.

It's amazing how, when I found Curt mid-ménage, I felt nothing but anger and irritation, but the absolute devastation I feel right now at the possibility that what I feel for Liam is all a magical lie is enough to rob me of air.

I pull out my phone and check the time, quickly calculating the time difference before calling Marie.

"Hey, love," she says excitedly. "Still living your best Irish adventure life?" I've been keeping Marie up to date on the Liam front.

She nearly made me dead in one ear when I told her I took her advice and quote-unquote hit that. Crazy ass woman screamed, probably fist pumped the air too.

"It's going," I say, choking back my tears.

"Oh, babe, what's wrong? Do I need to fly over there and put a boot up someone's ass? I will put a bitch down; you just say the word, and I'm on a plane."

She'd do it too.

I laugh as a few tears slip down my cheeks. "No. We are not wasting our bail funds on my stupidity."

"Don't you talk about my friend like that," Marie says fiercely.

"It's true," I say as the tears start to freefall. "I was stupid, and I-I-I caught feelings for Liam."

"Oh, honey. What happened?"

I take a few breaths, trying to figure out how to explain everything without sounding like I'm crazy or betraying Liam and his people's secret. I settle for a broad overview.

"Curt figured out where I'd be. Liam and I were wandering around the festival shopping at the artisan stalls when he found us. He was such a fucking dick, making a scene."

"Goddamn motherfucker. I told you he was a dickwad," Marie seethes.

"Yeah. Total dickhead," I chuckle. "So I basically told him to fuck off, but before that, Liam said something about he'd have a chance to win me back before midnight. Like, what does that even mean?"

Marie is quiet for a minute. "Did you ask him?" She says softly.

"Yes? I mean, he said a lot of things and that he loved me and —"

"Whoa, whoa, whoa! He said he loves you?"

"Yes," I croak as a wave of fresh tears streams down my face.

"And how do you feel about him?"

"I'm one hundred percent falling in love with him."

"Well, at least you're not in denial about that," she says.

"Excuse me?" I say, temporarily startled out of my tears.

"Piper, my bestie, my person in life, I know you better than anyone on this planet. Every time you have called since you met him, there's been a happiness in your voice I haven't heard in ages. And every phone call, that happiness grows.

I could tell you felt something for him. I was just hoping you weren't in denial about it, cause we were gonna have a come-to-Jesus talk if that was the case. Now I just want to know, do you believe him?"

"I don't know," I say, even though my initial reaction is to say I want to.

"Well, you need to figure that out. Until you do, don't do anything rash."

"Okay. I think, I think I'm going to just find a cafe and think. Thanks for shouldering my temporary mental breakdown," I say, trying to keep more tears at bay.

"Anytime, love. Call me back if you need to. I love you."

"Love you, too," I say, hanging up.

I wander a bit longer until I find a cafe. I order a coffee and sit out on the stone patio, watching the crowds gather for the parade. Right now, I'd be in that crowd with Liam, bubbling with excitement, had Curt not fucked everything up.

Pain radiates in my chest thinking of him. His smile and his laugh. The way he looks at me, how happy he is just to hold my hand. And the way he makes love to me, words spoken both in the heat of passion and the quiet after, while he holds me.

I really do love him. But is it real?

"May I join you? All the tables are full," a musical female voice asks by my side.

I look up to see a stunning woman with long, braided blonde hair and golden skin standing next to me with a kind smile. She's dressed in snug jeans and a cream sweater that highlights her green eyes.

"Oh, of course," I say, gesturing for her to take a seat opposite me.

We sit quietly for a few moments, and I begin to slip back into my own internal debate.

"Penny for your thoughts," she says in that lovely and

comforting Irish accent I've come to love during my adventures. When I turn to her, I catch the faint glimmer of wings in the last rays of the setting sun.

"You're a" I look around, then lean in to whisper, "fae."

Her wings solidify for a fraction of a second as she gives me an enchanting smile.

"I am. My name is Esmeralda. It's nice to finally meet you, Piper. Liam talks nonstop about you," she says.

"Did he send you?" I ask, slightly defensive.

Her smile drops a fraction as she shakes her head. "No, he didn't. I was in the market when that cretin harassed you. When you left, I went to check on Liam, and he told me he confessed his nature to you. When I saw you sitting here so sad, I couldn't help but stop and speak with you." There's genuine concern in her voice that makes me pause.

"And what would you say?" I ask.

"That what he said was true. He is a Gancanagh. His nature is to seduce women and men with his magic. But when he tells you that his magic doesn't work on you, he's telling you the truth. I'm a healer among my people. Liam came to me thinking his magic was broken.

Every time he spent time with you, he would try and use his magic and his charms, but nothing would work. He kept coming back to me, gushing about this incredible woman that he was over the moon for who was immune to his magic.

Without his magic, he got to know you, and you got to know him. And he fell completely in love with you. The reason his magic doesn't work on you is because you're the missing piece of his soul."

"What?" I ask her, confused.

"Let me ask you. How do you feel about him?"

"I fell in love with him, too," I say automatically. It was my initial reaction when talking to Marie. "I miss him," I say as tears begin to fall down my face, and I rub the ache in my chest.

Esmeralda smiles at me. "That ache you're trying to rub away? It's real. As real as the chair that's holding you up and the magic that brought you here. And he's somewhere in that crowd feeling that same ache."

"He is?" I hiccup on a sob.

"He is. Time is ticking away, and midnight will be here soon. What are you going to do?"

I push back out of the chair and stand, nearly knocking the table over.

"I have to find him," I say, wiping my tears. "Thank you, Esmeralda. I hope—I hope that we see each other again."

She gives me another enchanting smile. "I do too. Now go get your fae."

I leave the cafe as quickly as possible. I brush past countless people, searching for Liam. The festival is in full swing as the parade marches down the main thoroughfare.

"Liam," I yell into the crowd desperately. "Liam," I scream louder over the noise, praying by some miracle he hears me.

"Piper," a voice calls.

I turn desperately in a circle searching for the voice. Did I imagine it?

"Piper," the voice calls again. I run in the direction of my name. I come to a halt in the middle of an intersection where there's a break in the parade. My heart plummets when I see Curt standing on one street corner.

"I've been looking all over for you, Piper," Curt says.

"Piper." I turn quickly to see Liam watching from the opposite side of the street as the clock strikes midnight. His wings are on full display, which, given the elaborate costumes, means he fits right in.

"Liam," I whisper, taking in his disheartened expression.

"This guy again. Jesus, what a freak show with the costume." I hear Curt say over my shoulder, "Come on, Piper, let's go." I vaguely register his words.

I take a step toward Liam. Then another, until I'm running and jumping into his waiting arms.

"Piper," he breathes my name as he holds me close.

"I love you, too," I say before kissing him with everything I have. He returns my passion tenfold, spinning me around in circles happily.

"I love you, Piper. So much. I love you so much. Does this mean you believe me?"

I laugh through happy tears. "Since it's after midnight and you're still looking at me like I hung the moon and that you love me, yes, I believe you."

"Thank God," he says, kissing me once more.

When we break apart, I slide down his body, clasping his hands. "What now?" I ask.

"We go and catch the parade and say so long to Samhain. Tomorrow, we decide on our next adventure," he says, wrapping me in his wings.

"Sounds perfect to me."

About the Author

Maison De Loup is a pen name for a wild, witchy mom who after years of writing for fun, was finally not so gently encouraged to publish. When she's not hiding from the insane heat in the outer ring of Hell, known as Texas, you can find her baking, hanging with her friends, and family enjoying a mixed drink, or reading a smutty book.